There was once a bear with a magic pencil…

Wherever Bear goes he takes his magic pencil
with him. If ever he has a problem he just
draws his way out of trouble.

Often, when I go into schools to talk to
children, I encourage them to make up a new
Bear story with me. They are brilliant at it.

This Bear story is one I have created with the help
of some wonderfully talented children who entered
a competition run by The Sun newspaper.

Thank you to all the children who entered this
competition and proved that all youngsters can
draw and make up stories. And that we all possess
a wonderful ability to create when we sharpen our
magic pencils!

Anthony Browne

Anthony Browne
Children's Laureate (2009-2011)

Photograph © Jon Cartwright 2009

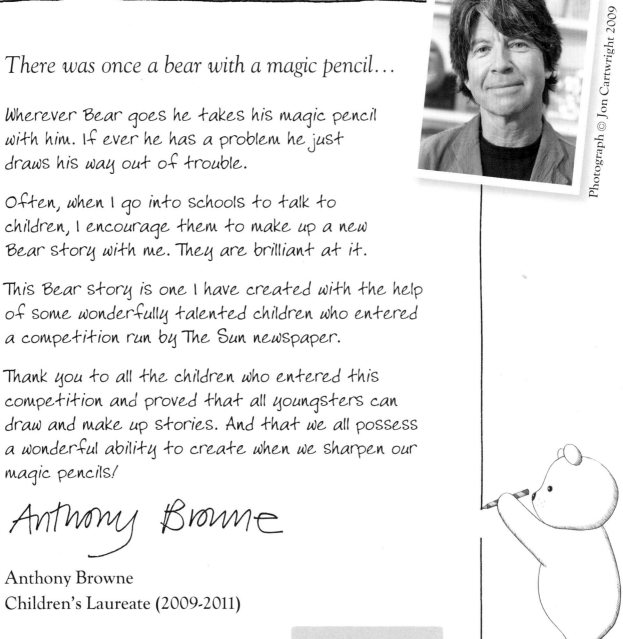

The images and stories used to make this book were created by the
following competition winners and runners-up.
Their images can be seen on the pages listed by each name.

WINNERS

Olivia Allen-Hall: p19-22 (honey, bee, tree, flowers)

Holly Edwards: p26-29 (panda, monkey, dolphins)

Jorja Glover: p17-19, 28 (giant, tree)

Alfie Graves: p15-18, 28-29 (whale, shorts)

Betty-Ann Hickey: p21-22, 25, 28-29 (polar bears, globe)

Faye Jackson: p8-10, 28, front cover (wolf, zigzags)

Elvy McCrudden: p23-26, 29 (dragons, parachute)

Ben Merson: p8-19, 21-23, 25-29, cover (butterflies, band)

Gracie Steele: p9, 11-13, 20-21, 28-29 (snake, bees, lettering, pogo stick)

Emma Wilbourne: p11, 13-14, 29, front cover (lion)

RUNNERS-UP

Oliver Baker: p2, 30 (spider)

Donny Bolt: back cover (lettering)

Billy Davies: p2, 30 (white bear with red pencil and red tie)

Monique Devaux: p2, 30, back cover (bear with light bulb)

Alex Doree: p3, 5, 31 (owl)

Tiegen Goodfellow: p2-3, 30-31 (penguin, bear with brown body)

Jennifer Lambert: p3, 31 (white bear with white pencil, princess)

Florrie Malcolm: p3, 31 (big brown bear)

Jake Marsden-Hirst: p3, 31 (dragon with bear)

Etienne Michels: p3, 31 (digger)

Ashton Nichols: p2, 30 (pirates, stripy bird, bear and spaceship)

Ceiran O'Donnell: p2-3, 30-31 (tractor, brown bear in red tie)

Esha Parmar: p2, 5, 30 (bears holding paws, carousel)

Lewis Reid: p2-3, 30-31 (dragon with black spikes, balloon)

Emily Rycroft: p2, 30 (bear with black legs)

Bethen Simpson: p3, 31 (butterfly, bear with wings)

Arthur Smith: p2-3, 30-31 (sitting bear, bird on chair)

Ellie Spivey: p3, 31 (bear with umbrella)

Freddie Wing: p2, 30 (bird in nest, rocket, gorilla)

Lois Wood: p2-3, 30-31 (bird and rainbow)

First published in paperback in Great Britain by HarperCollins Publishers Ltd, in association with
News Group Newspapers Ltd, a subsidiary of News International Limited in 2010
Illustrations by Anthony Browne first published in *The Little Bear Book* (1988) and *A Bear-y Tale* (1989) by
Hamish Hamilton Children's Books. Reproduced with permission of Penguin Books Ltd

3 5 7 9 10 8 6 4

ISBN: 978-0-00-738220-0

HarperCollins Children's Books is a division of HarperCollins Publishers Ltd.
News Group Newspapers Ltd is a subsidiary of News International Ltd.

Text copyright © HarperCollins Publishers Ltd and News Group Newspapers Ltd 2010
Illustrations copyright © Anthony Browne 1988, 1989, 2010
Additional illustrations copyright © HarperCollins Publishers Ltd and News Group Newspapers Ltd 2010

The Sun and The Sun Logo are registered trademarks of News Group Newspapers Ltd.

Visit our website at: www.harpercollins.co.uk

Visit The Sun website at: www.thesun.co.uk

Created and designed by The StoryWorks
www.thestoryworks.me.uk

Printed in Great Britain by Martins the Printers

You can see more of Bear's adventures in *Bear Hunt* published by Puffin Books.

Bear's Magic Pencil

Anthony Browne
and Friends

HarperCollins *Children's Books*

Bear was walking in the forest.
Suddenly...

...out jumped a wolf, licking his lips.
"What's that?" the wolf asked.
"It's my magic pencil," said Bear.

The magic pencil began to move up
and down and all over the wolf.
Zigzag marks appeared and the wolf...

...disappeared!
The wolf was scribbled out.
And Bear walked on.

SSSSSSSSSS!
A snake came slithering towards him.
Watch out, Bear!

Quickly, he used his magic pencil to draw a pogo stick.
Boing! Boing! Boing!
Bear bounced right over the snake.

GRRRRR! Bear heard a growling noise.
A hungry lion appeared.
Run, Bear, run!

But Bear drew some juicy meat
and threw it into the trees.
And the lion ran after it.

Bear walked on.
After a while he came to a lake.
"Coming for a swim?" asked a whale.

Bear drew himself some
swimming shorts.

SPLASH!
He swam right across the lake
and got out on the other side.

Bear met a sad giant. "No one will be my friend
because I'm too big," he said.
Bear drew a very tall apple tree.

The giant smiled. "Would you like an apple?"
"Yes, please," said Bear. "Apples are my favourite."
And Bear walked on.

Bear heard a buzzing. Honey!
A bee landed on Bear's nose.
Bear nearly dropped his pencil!

Quickly, he drew some flowers.
While the bees were busy,
Bear ate the honey.

Some other bears had smelled the honey too.
"We used to live at the top of the world in a land
of ice and snow," said the polar bear family.

"One day, the sky broke and the sun melted the ice.
Now we have to look for somewhere new to live."
Bear had a think. He drew a dragon.

Bear climbed on to
the dragon's back.
WHOOOSH!
Bear zoomed to the
top of the world.

He drew a new land
of ice and snow and
a bandage over the
broken sky. The polar
bears could go home.

Then Bear drew
himself a parachute.

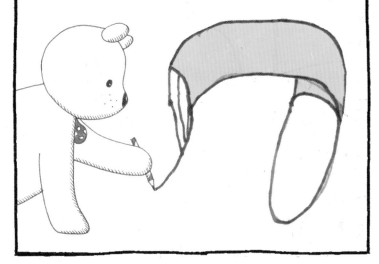

Down... down... down... floated Bear.
When he reached the ground, a panda was waiting
for him. Bear was shocked when the panda told him
about all the other animals who were

disappearing from the world because
their homes were being destroyed.
Bear had an idea.
He started to draw...

Bear drew bottle-nosed dolphins and
orang-utans and mountain gorillas and all
the endangered animals he could think of.

"Just in time," said Bear.
Then Bear saw a bear band.
He drew himself some drums and joined in.

About the Competition

Children's Laureate, Anthony Browne, has collaborated with the nation's number one newspaper, The Sun, and budding author-illustrators to create an exciting and unique picture book, combining his classic character – the bear with the magic pencil – with art and stories from the winning entries.

Anthony Browne started the story of a bear with a magic pencil, and children aged eight and under were invited to join in and complete the story as part of a national competition in The Sun.

There were a huge number of entries from all over the UK. The judging was carried out by bestselling children's writer Julia Donaldson (author of *The Gruffalo*), footballer Theo Walcott, BAFTA-winning children's TV writer Sarah Ball and Anthony himself, and aided by HarperCollins Publishers and The Sun team. Ten winners and twenty runners-up were selected.

Anthony then took the winning ideas and pictures and they were woven together and used to create a brand-new story. Where possible, phrases and storylines are the children's own clever inventions and you will see some fabulous pictures drawn by children as young as four years old. Anthony's artwork is taken from existing Bear stories and there are also some brand new Bear drawings he has specially created. The result is this fabulous picture book!

Anthony Browne, HarperCollins and The Sun are donating all royalties, totalling 10% of the publisher's proceeds from the sales of this book, to Rainbow Trust Children's Charity. (Registered charity: 1070532)

The post of Children's Laureate is administered by the independent reading charity Booktrust.

Congratulations to all the children whose work is featured!

Theo Walcott, Julia Donaldson and Anthony Browne
Photograph by Dan Jones